Early Writings

I am Fisher Stephens. My age is 17, and I have autism. I do not talk, because it is very hard to make my mouth say the words that fly from my head. I can type, so I do that. I like to type because it helps me become free to let out the pictures in my head. I see many pictures all the time. Sometimes it is hard for me to slow them down. Dad gives me medicine. It helps. Sometimes the pictures fly in my head so fast that I have to shake my hands and make some grunting noises. People look at me when that happens. I take medicine to help me calm down too.

My dad has the name Paul. My mom is not living anymore. I am not sure how she stopped living this life, but she was sick for a very long time. Dad says she is fine now, and we will live together again someday. I miss mom. Before she got so sick, she would read to me. I liked that. When I was really little she would make a soft place in bed with lots of blankets. We would watch my favorite movies and cuddle. We would eat lots of snacks and popcorn. Usually, I would fall asleep in bed, feeling safe with mom by my side. Every kid should know that feeling. Mom had a lot of love to give, but she wore out before she could give it all. I did not like to go in her room when she was very sick. Her room felt dark and cold to me. I am happy her sickness is all gone now, but I miss all the love she gave me.

People and Autism

I notice many things about people. I listen to the sounds their shoes make when they walk. I look at the color of their clothes. I don't know why, but now that I'm 17, I like to look at pretty girls' legs. One time, I went up to a very pretty girl at the store, and bent over to look closer at her pretty legs. Dad had to tell me not to do this. I do not stare anymore, but I really like girls' legs.

I watch people's faces as they talk on phones. Some people get very big eyes when they talk on the phone. Some people smile and laugh when they are on the phone. Some people yell into their phones. However, most people do not talk, or smile, or laugh when they are walking right next to somebody. This seems strange to me. Phones are nice, but I think people do not pay attention to each other very much.

Autism is part of me. I feel it inside me. Dad says it is part of what makes me special. Sometimes I do not feel special. Sometimes when we see people we know at the big store, they see us, and walk away from us in a hurry. It makes my dad sad, and me too. One time, at the big store, I bumped my head really hard. I was little, and it hurt a lot. I could not stop crying because the hurting made lots of bad pictures fly in my head, and many bad colors too. Dad tried to calm me down, but I started screaming and holding my ears. A lady said to my dad, very loud, that he should take me into the bathroom and "teach me a lesson" about how to behave. I do not really know why she said that, but it really seemed to hurt my dad. He looked at her with a mad face, but he had tears in his eyes. That is the only time I have seen my dad cry.

Another time at the store, I was upset, and shaking my hands a lot while I made noises. It was very loud in the store that day, and there were too many people. I was tired and did not feel good.

An old lady looked at my dad and said, "What is wrong with him."

Dad said, "Absolutely nothing."

We just walked away from her. I do not feel special when people look at me and say dark things.

I DO feel special sometimes though. I feel very special when I get visits from my friend. He has the name Michael. He always comes to visit at night. I used to think I was sleeping and Michael was a night picture in my head. But now I know that is not true. Every time Michael comes to visit, there is a bright light outside the window of my room. He never uses the door. Michael comes in right through the wall.

Michael looks different from most people. His skin is very smooth and his eyes are big black circles. His color is light blue. Michael is very kind and makes me feel calm and happy. My hands do not shake when he is here. Most of all, I like that Michael can talk to me in my head. He does not need his lips. He thinks things and they go into my head. I hear them, but his mouth does not move. Even better than that, I can say something in my head and he hears it. Many times we have talked this way most of the night. Like my dad, Michael tells me I am very special. He says I am important for the future and he needs to teach me many things. I am not sure why this is, but I like it. I feel safe and warm with Michael. He seems to know me very well. When we talk, the pictures in my head are slow and happy. I have noticed that since Michael has been coming to visit me, I am better at using words. I can think of more words, and it is easier to type them. I still cannot talk with my lips. I wish I could.

Thomas the Tank Engine

I love trains. I really love Thomas the Tank Engine. Even though I am 17, I do not think Thomas is silly. The thing I love best about Thomas and his friends is the colors. They have very bright colors. Colors make sense to me. I can organize colors in my head, and that relaxes me. I also like numbers. Almost all of the Thomas engines have numbers. Numbers help me organize things in my head too. I can think of James. He is the red, number 5 engine. Gordon is the big blue, number 4 engine. Numbers are good, but colors are better. I look at colors when we drive in the car too. Stop lights are red, or green, or yellow. Red means you have to stop. Green means you can go. Dad says yellow means be careful, but sometimes when the light is yellow, he drives very fast, so I am not so sure about yellow.

Dad

My dad is my best buddy. We do everything together. I really like watching movies with dad. We go to the Roxy Theater, and the mall. We eat lunch out. I like to have pizza and noodles on Saturday. Saturday is my favorite day. We go to all my favorite stores. We do not buy things very much. Sometimes I get a new Thomas engine, or a new book. Mostly, we look at people. The people we see do not seem to be as happy as we are. They look like they are sad, and in a hurry.

They all look down at their phones and do not talk to each other. They seem to want to only buy things. My dad and I just like to be together.

One of my favorite things about dad is every night, we flop on the couch every night to watch a movie together. We call it "big flop." The dogs usually lay down with us too. Dad likes to pick the movie. He likes movies as much as I do. We both like "Wallace and Gromit" a lot. It makes us feel like we are kind of watching ourselves. Dad is Wallace, and I am Gromit. That is my favorite time. When we lay down on the couch every evening, I do not worry about anything. I do not think dad does either. We are just happy and comfortable. I think too many people try to make themselves feel happy by owning a lot of stuff. It does not seem to make them happy. Just being with my dad makes me happy.

Sometimes, when we walk, we see people who do not have a home. They live on the street. I worry about them getting enough food to eat. I worry more about them in winter when it is so cold outside. My dad always stops to talk to them, and gives them some money for food.

"We have to help those people who do not have as much as we do, Fisher," he says. "It's just what people should do for each other."

Dad is bald. I do not understand why I have hair on my head, but my dad does not. I like his bald head. It is very smooth. When we watch TV, I rub my dad's head. It calms me down, and I think it calms dad down too. Dad also has a beard. How can he have no hair on his head, but hair grows very much on his face? Sometimes, he uses a razor on my face. I only get a few hairs on my face, but dad has millions.

Dad likes to cook too. He makes me many good things to eat. When mom was living, she and dad cooked together. It made them very happy. Mom was messy in the kitchen, and dad was always cleaning up after her. They laughed a lot when they cooked together, and sometimes they got silly. One time, they had an accident. They dropped potato salad on one of the cats. The cat was very mad, but the dogs came over and licked the potato salad off the cat. It made us all laugh. Dad still likes to cook, but I do not think it makes him as happy as it did when mom was alive.

Dad also loves to walk. We take long walks by the river. It is nice and quiet. My dad talks to me, even though I cannot talk back to him. He knows what I am thinking. When it is hot, dad takes me to Dairy Queen for a hot dog. He says it is for me to get a snack, but he always gets ice cream too. So, I think it is as much fun for him as it is for me. Wherever dad goes, he takes me with him. I am glad we go everywhere together. Some kids in my special class stay home a lot. Their parents do not even take them to the store. Home is nice in the evening when I get tired, but during the day, I like to be out and busy with dad. I also love school. I really wish school was every day. Sometimes dad and I will just ride in the car and listen to music. I like lots of kinds of music. I listen to Johnny Cash a lot. He is one of my dad's favorites. We also like AC/DC. They are loud, and it makes a good feeling go up my back when we listen to them.

Animals

We have many animals at our house, but I am not so sure why. I think my dad really likes animals. We have two dogs. They are called Lily and Bingley. Lily is brown and Bingley is white. I think Lily is a pug. Her face is black and smashed in. She is little, and she has a curly tail that curves around like the top of an ice cream cone at Dairy Queen. Sometimes Lily is very bad, but my dad lets her do anything she wants to. She likes to get into my closet and get my underwear. She runs around the house with it, and dad and I chase her. She likes to be chased. It is kind of fun, but sometimes she makes holes in my undies. Bingley is white. He has fluffy hair, like a lamb. He looks like a Doctor Seuss dog. He is little, but he thinks he is very big. He barks a lot, even when nothing is there. I think he might

be crazy. My dad calls him "the white wolf," since he thinks he is big and tough.

Bingley behaves better than Lily now that he is older. He was also very bad when

he was a young dog. He used to get inside the dish washer. He used to steal my

food too. He is very soft, and I like to pet him.

Dogs spend much time wiggling. I feel funny when things wiggle, and not such

a good kind of funny. Dogs make a lot of noise too.   One time I hit the door

chimes when I was walking to my room. The dogs thought somebody was at the

door. They barked so loud, they made the door chimes ring!

I told them in my head, "Dogs, nobody is at the door."

They would not stop. I thought maybe dogs could understand my head-talking.

But mostly, I think dogs just wiggle and bark.   Since my dad likes the dogs, I try to

like the dogs too.

Now that mom is not living anymore, the dogs sleep with dad. They get very

close to him. I think my dad is lonely, and that is why he lets the dogs sleep with

him. They push against him and make him all curled up in strange shapes. Dad

does not seem to mind. He holds the dogs and talks nicely to them. He talks to

them a lot like he talked to mom when she was very sick. He would say things to make her laugh, and she did not mind her sickness as much. I think talking to the dogs makes my dad feel better since he does not have mom to talk to anymore. Anyway, I am very glad the dogs do not sleep with me.

We have three cats too. They are Ivy, Violet and Edward. Ivy is very big. She is black and brown and grey. The brown in her fur reminds me of peanut butter topping on ice cream. Ivy is nice and likes it when someone pets her. Even though she is very fat, she has a tiny voice, like a kitten. This makes me laugh. Violet is also a fat cat. She is white and grey and has the same kind of peanut butter color in her fur too. She is very loud and always wants to eat. She likes to be petted, but sometimes, when I am petting her, she gets a funny look on her face and wraps her whole body around my hand and arm. Her claws are sharp and it hurts. I didn't mean to, but one time when she did that, I threw her across the room. She just landed on her feet and started licking her paws. I think she is kind of loony. Edward is an older cat. He is not as fat. He is grey and likes to go outside to hunt. One time, dad opened the door to let Edward inside and Edward had a live bat in his mouth! He opened his mouth and the bat started to fly around the dining room table. Dad gave me a tennis racket, and we both chased the bat around the table. Finally, after we got very much tired, dad opened the door and the bat flew out of the house. I think Edward had fun watching us chase the bat.

Cats do many other strange things. Our cats sometimes run very fast through the house for no reason. Then, they stop very fast and swish their tales. After they stop swishing, they suddenly start to lick themselves. Sometimes cats have very big eyes. Their eyes glow at night. Cats seem to really like nighttime. Sometimes when I am trying to sleep, the cats are running very fast through the house and slamming into things. Usually, Edward likes to sleep with me. He is older and calmer...usually. He rubs against me to be petted, and then he will stick his butt in my face! I do not know why cats do that at all! My dad says it is because Edward loves me, but I am very happy that people do not do that when they love me.

Jonah

There is a boy at school who does not like me. He is Jonah. I get feelings about people when I meet them. Sometimes when I meet a person, I get warm, and see good colors like orange or yellow. Sometimes I feel cold, and see black or other dark colors around the person. Jonah is a person who makes me feel very cold and makes me see dark. He knocks my hat off every day and calls me "the sped."

I do not understand what a sped is, but I think it is a bad name. I tried not wearing a hat, but Jonah tapped me hard on the head, and still called me "the sped." Jonah does not seem to need to be, but he is in my special class. Maybe he is just there because he is mean. The other kids say Jonah is rich and spoiled. I always thought food got spoiled when it was old. Maybe Jonah is like very old cheese.

Jonah does not seem to have any friends. He would have more friends if he did not always say mean things, but everyone says he has always been like that, and cannot stop. I do not know why, but I feel like someday Jonah will fight with me. He is mean to other kids too. There is a boy named Samuel who has dark skin. He is in my special class and he is very nice. I like to be with him, because he speaks in a soft voice to me. Jonah makes fun of Samuel's dark skin. Jonah has gotten in trouble for this many times, but he still does it. He called Samuel a word that I am not allowed to say. It must be the worst word in the world, because when Jonah said it, all the kids and teachers got very quiet. Everyone in the room had an open mouth, and looked at Jonah. Jonah thought it was funny. He was smiling and laughing. I looked over at Samuel. His eyes were very sad. The Principal took Jonah away, and we did not see him again for a long time. I typed it all out for my dad because I was upset. Dad said it is stupid to make fun of a person's skin. He said that it makes him mad that pictures of Jesus always show him with white skin. He told me Jesus had dark skin because of where he lived. Dad explained that many people who live in our town think that their ideas are the only ones that matter, and everyone should think like they do.

"Fisher don't ever be afraid to think for yourself and do what is right," he said. "It's easy to do what is popular, but sometimes it takes guts to do what is right."

Dad was quiet for a minute.

"Fisher," he said. "I know this is hard to do, but try to be good to Jonah. I think he is hurting pretty badly inside. His dad does not really pay much attention to him, and his mom moved away when Jonah was very young."

I thought about how much I missed my mom. It made sense that Jonah was angry and sad. Most of the time when I saw Jonah, he was all alone. Jonah's dad was always buying him stuff to try to make up after they had a fight. They fought a lot. My dad has gotten upset with me a few times, but we never fight. I do play some jokes on him though.

One time, my dad was getting ready to take a shower. He remembered that his clean clothes were downstairs in the dryer. He ran to the basement, naked, to get his clean clothes. After he ran downstairs, I locked the basement door. The only way to get back into the house was out through the basement and up the front stairs. Finally, I let him back upstairs after he banged on the door a few times and called my name. When I opened the door, I pointed at him and laughed hard. He was kind of red, but he laughed too, and told me I was a great comedian.

Mary

My best friend at school is Mary. Mary can talk, but she can only see out of one eye. She is in many of my classes. Like me, she needs extra help from special teachers. Mary is older than I am, so she kind of takes care of me. Sometimes when my dad has to work late, or do something else, he asks Mary to stay with me. She is always nice to me. I always get a warm feeling around her, and I see many different shades of yellow around her head. She is very pretty too. Sometimes when she is joking with me, I see a pink circle around her head. She knows I like to joke with her, and I think it makes her extra happy to make me laugh. Mary gets very angry when Jonah is mean to me. She picks up my hat when Jonah knocks it off, and gives me a hug.

She says, "Don't worry Munchkin. He's just lonely and sad."

She calls me Munchkin and it makes me smile. We both love to watch The Wizard of Oz. Sometimes Mary comes to my house and we watch the Wizard of Oz together. It is one of our favorite movies, except for the bad flying monkeys. When it is time for the monkeys, Mary and I hide under a big blanket, or sometimes we go get a snack. I feel best when I am with Mary, Samuel, my dad, and Michael. Michael has the brightest colors I have ever seen around anyone. It looks like a rainbow.

Noise

Some noises bother me. Singing bothers me because it is too busy. I hear all the voices and cannot separate them. That bothers me and I have to cover my ears. I like to sing, but when other people sing in big groups, the noise is too much. It is kind of like wiggling dogs. Other noises bother me too. I do not like the vacuum. It has a sound that feels like something sharp is going into my ear. Vacuums hurt. Dad knows this, and warns me when he is going to use the vacuum. Since I do not like it, he calls it the "evil machine." I go in my TV room and close the doors when the "evil machine" is running. I think the cats also think it is the "evil machine." When the "evil machine" gets too loud, I put on a pair of headphones. I do not listen to music like most people do with headphones. I just wear them to help block noise that hurts.

I love the sound of trains. When dad and I stand by the tracks, we wave at the engineer. Most of the time, he will blow his horn. My dad does not understand why big train noises do not bother me, but the vacuum does. Train sounds are happy, but vacuum sounds are bad.

The sound of a fan is a good sound too. I like to put my head right in front of a fan, or an air conditioner. It feels nice and cool, and it sounds nice too. It is hard for me to be around crying babies. I really get upset when I hear babies cry. The noise hurts, but most of all, I feel sad for babies. They are little, and I think the world scares them sometimes.

Pacing

I pace a lot. It is one of the only ways I can work out all my energy. I do not understand why I have so much energy. It seems like enough energy for at least two people. At least, that is what my dad says. If I can't fall asleep, I get out of bed and pace. A lot of the time, I pace while I eat. Sometimes when I do not feel good, I pace. I really hate having a sore throat. It hurts all the time, especially when I swallow. Most of all, it bothers me that I cannot reach in and make my throat feel better by scratching it. So, I pace even more when I have a sore or scratchy throat.

My pacing is the one thing that seems to bother my dad. He is very patient with me. He does not mind my hand-flapping. He does not mind my strange noises, but my pacing makes him feel stressed. I think it is because he knows I am upset, and he cannot do much to help me. That makes him pace, and then it is kind of like a parade going around our house. Dad and I pace around the house together, and the animals lay on the chairs and watch us. That seems kind of funny to me.

My First Lesson with Michael

I remember the pictures that come into my head. I remember them forever. I have a very strong picture in my head about the first night Michael came to visit me. I was sleeping and a very bright light outside my window woke me up. I was not afraid. I felt very good and warm inside. When I woke up, Michael was already talking to me inside my head.

He said, "Fisher…I am Michael, your friend. I am here to bring you happiness."

Even though I still could not use my mouth, it felt very nice to be able to talk to somebody. We talked inside our heads for a long time. Michael told me that people who have autism, and other disabilities, are very important for the future.

He started to teach me right away. He showed me how he used his thoughts to move things around. He moved my laundry basket across the room. He thought very hard, closed his eyes and held out one hand. The laundry basket slid back to where it had been. He told me to sit in a chair by my desk. I did. He closed his eyes and put his hand out. Soon, I began to go up in the air in my chair. Then, he moved me back into my bed. This was so much fun! I could not believe I could do this, but Michael told me to try. I closed my eyes and thought really hard about my stuffed rabbit, Mr. Bugs. I tried to lift him, but nothing happened. Michael told me to do it again but to pretend the rabbit was alive. I did...but still nothing. Michael put his hand on my head and made me calm. He said I had to breathe in and count slowly. Then, he told me to breathe out and count backwards slowly.

He pointed to my cat, Edward, "Try it on him."

I thought about Edward very hard. I imagined him flying through the air from where he was sleeping. I breathed deeply in and out and counted as I breathed. I closed my eyes and held out my hand, just the way Michael had done. Finally,

Edward lifted just a little bit. I still had trouble believing I was doing this! I tried again and did everything Michael told me to. Edward lifted into the air and drifted across the room. He landed gently at the bottom of my bed. He did not even wake up. Michael and I laughed. (The next morning, when Edward did wake up, he looked confused.)

Michael told me not to use the power out in the world yet. He said I had to wait and I would know when to use it. Right now, he said I should not show anyone, and practice using the power in my own house. He told me not even to show dad or Mary. I thought it was strange that Michael seemed to know everyone in my life. He talked about dad, Mary, Samuel…and Jonah. He also seemed to know all about everything in my life and my autism.

"Some parts of your brain do not work like everyone else's," he said. "However, you have some parts of your brain that allow you to do amazing things."

"Why are you helping me to learn these things?" I asked.

"We need to help others. It's just the right thing to do," he answered.

He smiled and told me to get some sleep. He walked through the wall and was gone.

Practicing

Many months went by. I did not see Michael during that time. I practiced using my new power. I lifted flowerpots and put them back down gently. I made my stuffed animals fly across the room at the dogs when they wiggled too much. That made me laugh. Sometimes Bingley would chase the stuffed animals. Lily just looked kind of scared. One day, while Edward was eating his crunchy cat food, I made his dish go up in the air. He batted at it with his paw. Cat crunchies flew everywhere and Edward ran off.

I tried moving bigger things too. One day, while dad was inside, I lifted the lawn mower. I really liked doing this, because the lawn mower makes a lot of noise, and it bothers me. I felt like playing a joke on dad. He went into the house to get his sunglasses so he could mow the grass. When he came back outside, I had "flown" the mower to the other side of the yard. He got a very strange look on his face when he came back outside. I tried to act like nothing was wrong.

One day, I decided to lift the car. At first, nothing happened. I sat down and got calm. I closed my eyes and lifted one hand. I imagined the car being lifted off the driveway. When I opened my eyes, the car was four or five feet off the ground, but it was drifting away across the street! I got scared, and it came crashing down. I had to do something to fix this! Michael told me when I had a hard time calming down, I had to think about my breathing. He said to count

slowly as I took a breath in and count slowly backwards as I let the breath out. I did this and it worked. I was very calm after a few breaths. I closed my eyes, and imagined the car flying back into the parking spot in the driveway. I imagined the car landing softly. When I looked, the car was gently coming back down in the place where dad always parked it. I smiled because I could feel this power growing inside me. I could also make myself calm down without my medicine. I did not flap my hands as much now that I had the power, and I could slow down the pictures in my head. I still could not talk with my mouth, but words started to come to me more easily. I typed all the time in great big sentences. Michael had said I was going to be important to the future. I was starting to feel important and kind of special.   **Frogs**

I have always liked frogs. They are peaceful and they do not hurt anyone…except bugs. We have a fish pond in our front yard. My dad likes to raise fish. I like fish too, but I really like the frogs that come to live in our ponds. I do not know how we got frogs. You have to have tadpoles to get frogs. We did not put tadpoles, or frog eggs, in our ponds, so where did the frogs come from? My dad says maybe a bird dropped some frog eggs into our pond and they grew. In school we grew tadpoles and watched them turn into frogs. Watching them change made me feel very good inside. I watched the tadpoles swim using their tails when they were little. As they grew, the tails disappeared and they grew legs and funny frog faces. Tadpoles transform into a brand new creature. Butterflies do this too, but I like frogs better because they can eat butterflies. I also love to listen to frogs. The noise makes me happy. We all change like tadpoles do, but people are slower. I feel like I am changing from a tadpole into something new, but I am not sure what yet. Maybe, I have been given special abilities to help others grow from a tadpole into a frog.

Michael's Return

Michael came back to see me last night. I was happy to see him since it had been a long time. We talked for a long time in our heads. At first, we just talked about fun, happy things, but then he got serious. He made me move things around the room for him to prove I had been practicing. Then, he had me stand up and walk to the wall of my bedroom. He walked through the wall, and then told me to try. At first, I kept hitting my nose on the wall. It was kind of funny, but it also hurt.

Michael told me to believe that the wall was not there at all. It only existed in my mind.

"There are many parts to this universe," he said. "Your room is only one dimension of this universe...Believe it is not there and it will not be."

I did not know what he meant, but I pretended the wall was all gone, and I walked through it. Outside, Michael stood under a bright light. He smiled and told me the time was coming soon when I would need to start using my powers. He told me to walk back into my room and go to sleep. I was surprised how easily I walked back through the wall. I looked out the window. Michael smiled and waved. Then, he disappeared.

Computers and Opera

I love computers. They make a lot of sense to me. You type in what you want, and they show it to you. When my brain starts to go too fast, I get on my computer, and I watch a movie at the same time. It keeps my brain very busy, so I don't mind that my brain is going too fast. I'm not sure if most people understand that about people with autism. Our brains go so fast that we have trouble concentrating on just one thing. It helps me to be calm if I have many things happening at once. Sometimes I get my dad's computer, and mine, and the television going at the same time. I type in both computers while I use the remote to watch different things on TV. I think it drives my dad nuts, because he can only do one thing at a time.

I also like to watch opera for the same reason. Operas have singing, acting, dancing and lots of colors and movement. One time, I watched a long opera. It was three hours long, but it made me very calm. It was in Italian, I think, so I didn't understand the words, but I really liked it. My dad teaches music, but he doesn't like opera, so that really made him crazy.

It Starts to Make Sense

Soon after my last visit from Michael, dad and I were at the store. I was looking at the Thomas engines in the toy section, and I heard a man yelling very loudly. He was yelling at a little boy. The boy was crying. The boy wanted to look at the Thomas engines too, but the man told him they were stupid. I think the bad man was the little boy's father. I looked very carefully at the man. He had black all around him, and I could tell the little boy was very scared of him. This man scared me too. I felt like I knew this little boy. It was kind of like I had seen a picture of him somewhere a long time ago. My dad was at the other end of the toys looking at something. I suddenly felt very brave, so I went over to the boy. He looked at me and stopped crying. I thought of the time at the store when I could not stop crying and the mean lady made my dad so sad and mad. This boy had big eyes that were almost black in the middle. He had black, curly hair and kind of dark skin. He was little, but he looked very strong. The boy started to smile at me. He got bright colors around him. Then, I was very surprised. The boy spoke to me in my head.

"Hello," he said. "I am David."

"I am Fisher. Please stop crying. I am here to bring you happiness." The words seemed to pour from my head without thinking. That is what Michael had said to me when we met.

Then, the boy's dad saw me and yelled again. This time, he yelled at me.

Don't bother with him kid...he can't talk," he told me. "My kid ain't right in the head."

I felt very sad. David's eyes were full of pain and sadness. I wanted to make him feel better. I started to get very mad at the bad man. I started to get pictures in my head that were going very fast, and they were not happy pictures. I saw scary things...monsters and scary faces. I saw red and lots of fire. The noises in my head started to get very loud and my hands started to shake.

The bad man looked at me and said, "Oh great! Another retard!"

I have never liked that word. I think it is like the word stupid, and I am not stupid. When people say it, it feels like a sharp knife going into my stomach. Now the bad man was laughing a mean laugh at both of us. David started to cry again. I wanted to do something. I remembered what Michael had said about knowing when to use the power. I believed with all my heart that now was the time.

I made my brain calm down by breathing slowly. I counted as I breathed in and counted as I breathed out. I breathed in again, and closed my eyes. I thought of my lessons with Michael. The bad man was in the car section, standing by cans of oil now. I tried really hard to make a can move, but I was still upset. I thought about the time I had moved the car...but still nothing. Then, I thought about Edward, my cat, flying through the air. I tried so hard to use the power, I thought my eyes might pop out. I took one last big breath and moved my hand quickly. At last, one can flew off the shelf and hit the man in his teeth, like a bullet. He screamed like a little girl. I breathed deeply again and concentrated more. POP! Another can hit the man.

"What the ...," he screamed, but that was all he got to say.

Several more cans smacked him in the face and in his private places. I thought about how I had lifted the car and walked through the wall. If I could do that, I knew I could make a few cans fly through the air. It worked, but not just a few cans fell. All the cans came down on the man, along with the shelves. There was a huge crash! It sounded like the time I heard a car slam into a wall. The man was laying on the floor under all the cans, making funny little noises. He sounded kind of like a sad puppy.

David was smiling at me. He came over to me and spoke to me in my head again. "Do you know Michael?"

"I know him very well,' I replied. "He visits me sometimes at night."

"Me too," he said.

It made me happy to know that somebody else knew Michael. I had still sometimes wondered if Michael had been a dream...or if maybe I was crazy. Now, I was sure Michael was real, and I knew the power was real. Most of all, I knew I was not alone. There were others like me. A pretty lady came running toward David and picked him up. I think it was his mom. She looked scared, but she seemed to be happy that David was OK. She looked angrily at the bad man. He was sitting up now. David smiled and waved to me as the lady carried him off.

I walked down the aisle to my dad. He had heard the noise.

"What was all the racket?" he asked. "You okay?"

I pointed to the man. A man who worked in the car section of the store was helping the man up. The bad man was yelling that he would sue the store.

"Seems like a charming guy," dad said. "Come on buddy. Let's go look at the movies."

I felt happy for a minute. The power had worked. I could control it. I had used it to help somebody who was a lot like me. I smiled and started to follow dad.

Then, I looked across the store to the televisions. Standing in the aisle was Jonah. He had been watching the whole thing. I stopped and watched him. He stared at me with black eyes. He looked different. He had on a long black coat. It looked to me as if he was standing in a cloud of black smoke. He looked very mad, but he had a scary kind of smile on his face. He held up his middle finger at me. I knew this was the bad finger. He blinked his eyes and moved his hand. A roll of duct tape flew off a shelf beside him and rolled over to my feet.

"Your time will come, Sped," he said to me.

What really scared me was that he said it to me in my head. His lips did not move. I shivered. Jonah had the power, and he could talk to me in my head. I felt very cold as I ran to catch up with my dad. I turned around, but Jonah was already gone. **Tribes**

I could not go to sleep that night. I was too scared of what Jonah might do to me in school the next day. What if Jonah wanted to fight me? Should I use the powers again? I felt very scared and my hands started to shake, even though I had just taken my medicine. I got up and started to pace. My dad was sleeping, so I tried to be quiet, but I paced very fast. I was glad to see a light outside of my window. Michael came into my room and sat on my bed.

"I know all about what happened tonight," he said calmly. "Don't worry. Jonah cannot hurt you. Your powers are much stronger than his."

"Michael," I asked. "Why do I have these powers?" "Why does Jonah have powers?" "What are we?"

"You are a member of the tribe Behira," he answered. "So are David, Samuel and Mary." "All people on Earth who have disabilities are people who have great power. Not all of them know it"

"Is Jonah in my tribe?" I asked.

"No…Jonah has chosen the tribe of Choshek."

Michael went on to tell me that these two tribes were of our choosing. We either chose the tribe of light, which is Behira, or we chose the tribe of darkness…Choshek. I told him I never remembered making a choice. He told me that we make the choice in our hearts. He said that Jonah was raised in a home where he was always looked at as a failure, because of his disability. His father would have nothing to do with him, and often told Jonah that he was stupid. This hardened Jonah's heart, and filled him with misery and hatred.

"He cannot defeat you, because light ALWAYS overcomes darkness in the end," Michael stated.

"But what do I do if he attacks me?" I had to ask.

"Try to turn and walk the other way, and do NOT become angry," Michael explained. "He is powerless unless you show anger. "That's why he could use his powers at the store…You were angry at David's father." "If he continues to attack you, use your powers, but you must control your anger. Try, by all means, to avoid fighting Jonah if you can. We may still be able to turn him around."

I asked about David. "His dad is mean, but David is very good. How can that be?"

Michael explained that David's mother was very kind and loving. David lived with her, but sometimes his dad would take David when he was not permitted to. That was why his mom had looked so scared and worried at the store.

I explained to Michael that I was feeling much different since I had found the power. Not only did I feel confident and strong, but words were coming to me much more clearly. I could type better, faster, and with smoother words. More words were moving smoothly through my head.

"That is because you are no longer a tadpole," he said. "You are transforming into a frog...a powerful frog"

I asked, "Am I the king of the Behira tribe?"

"No...that is David."

He told me he would come to visit me again soon. He put his hand on my shoulder and vanished. Now I felt tired and wanted to sleep. The next day at school, Jonah stayed away from me, but I watched him very carefully.

Practicing

One day, my dad was in the basement doing some work. I decided to have some fun practicing my powers. I lifted my shoes off of the bedroom floor and made them chase each other. I walked through the closet door and walked through all of my clothes hanging there. I sat on the floor in a meditation position Michael had shown me, and found I could slowly lift myself into the air, if I kept my eyes closed and kept my breathing steady.

All of the dogs and cats were in my room sleeping. I started my deep breathing again. I looked at Bingley and held out my hand. He shot up into the air! I stopped him about half way to the ceiling and held him there. I lifted Lily, the pug, up next. I held her and Bingley face to face about five feet in the air. They looked kind of funny, but they seemed to be having fun. Lily batted at Bingley with her front paws. Bingley woofed at her. Next, I lifted Ivy, the biggest cat. She was not happy. I circled her around the dogs like a satellite. Then, I did the same thing with the other two cats, Edward and Violet. At first, everything was fine. Then, both dogs started barking at the cats. The cats hissed, and their fur stood up on their backs. I stopped all of them and just held them all in mid-air. The barking and hissing stopped. I could hear my dad coming down the hall. I lowered the cats onto my bed, but I slipped and both dogs landed on top of my bedroom dresser. Dad walked in. The cats' fur was still standing up on their backs, and they were growling the way cats do when they are mad. The dogs just stood on top of my dresser looking kind of goofy.

"What happened to them?" Dad asked.

I just typed on my computer and tried not to smile. Dad looked confused and told me to get ready. We were going out for a walk. After he walked out of the room, I lowered the dogs to the floor and gave them a treat. I patted the cats, who were still mad. I walked over to my closet. Just for fun, I walked through the door. I stood in the dark closet for a minute, feeling very pleased with myself. I walked, through the door, back out into my room. Walking through things felt kind of strange and tingly. I liked it. As I walked out of my bedroom, I snapped my fingers, and my ball cap came flying after me. It landed perfectly on my head. It was good to have the power!

A Serious Talk

When Michael visited me the next time, he told me he needed to have a serious talk with me about my purpose. I sat on my bed, ready to listen. When Michael spoke to me in my head, it was a lot like reading a book. I not only heard his words, but saw very clear pictures, like those in an illustrated book.

"Fisher, I have told you many things. Your powers are getting very strong. Now, I have to tell you more about why you are so important."

I sat up straight. I felt a little nervous, a lot like the time dad had told me that mom was not living anymore.

Michael continued, "You are one of the most important members of the Behira tribe. There is a constant battle going on between the Behira and the Choshek. It has been going on for thousands of years. The Behira will always defeat the Choshek as long as there is more good on Earth than evil, but that is rapidly changing. The Choshek have been growing in numbers at a great rate over the last hundred years. Now, the numbers in each tribe are getting dangerously close."

I felt confused, "It doesn't seem like there are more mean people to me."

"There are many kinds of evil," Michael said, "not just people who are mean. There are people who worship money and power, and themselves. Have you noticed there are more people suffering and living on the streets?"

"Yes,"I said, " I see people asking for money when we go to the store."

"We must never ignore those who are suffering," Michael continued. The Choshek are greedy. They take more and more money from those who are in need, and from those who are trying to make an honest living. They do not care about the needy. The Choshek see the needy as a nuisance. They also think only of themselves, and of having power over others. They think they are the wisest and greatest beings on Earth, but they worship themselves. Do you know the word *ego* Fisher?"

"No," I replied.

"It is a word that describes the worst kind of evil," he said. "Ego means that you think of yourself always before others, or before anything else. It means that you think you are more important than others. The Choshek have made themselves into gods. That idea is very tempting to many people, but it is a terrible way to live. When you begin to live as a god, you create a terrible world of misery for yourself, and you end up living in the netherworld."

"Why don't we just let the Choshek go and live there?" I asked. "Couldn't we just live someplace nice and leave them where they end up?"

"If they continue to grow in power, they could pull everyone into the netherworld." Michael explained. "In fact, they will create the netherworld right here on Earth. Have you noticed how many people seem to live only to go out and spend money?"

"Yes," I said, "I see many people in a hurry to buy things at the mall. One time, I saw two women fighting over a sweater."

"That is a type of evil, Fisher, "Michael said. "People do not see it as evil, because everyone has been so encouraged to buy things. They think it is essential to buy lots of possessions, but it is really wrong. Clothing, jewelry, cars, nice houses, phones… any type of possession can become something that we worship and see as a necessity. Look at how many people have died in wars for oil. People feel they need to have their cars so badly, they will do anything to get more oil for their cars. Car companies make more and more cars because people feel they have to have them. Oil companies find more and more places to drill for oil so people can drive their cars more and more. Look at how much gasoline costs, but people drive their cars more and more, while ignoring people who are starving on the streets."

"Why do we have to have people like the Choshek?" I asked. "Why can't everyone get along and take care of each other?"

"Many centuries ago, there was a great war between the Choshek and Behira. The Choshek lost and lived in hiding for many years. They became more and more angry and bitter. Gradually, they began coming out into the world more and more. They tempted people by offering a life of money and pleasure. If someone tried to fight them, they would often ruin that person's life, and sometimes even kill them."

"That still happens today," I said.

"Yes,' Michael said. "The Choshek are more powerful now than ever. They are everywhere...government, the churches of all faiths, banks, and especially in the world of business."

I nodded my head in understanding. "We have to try to bring the world back into the light."

"That's right," said Michael.

I couldn't help but ask, "Why do people like me have to do this?"

"People who may be physically weak, or disabled, are strong in many other ways," Michael answered. "Did you ever hear the phrase *The meek shall inherit the Earth*?"

"Yes, I've heard that."

"You have your powers for that reason. People who are not disabled do not have the special powers you do. People like you, Fisher, must now rise up and become leaders in this world...and universe."

"Will there be another great war?" I asked.

"Perhaps, but we first must try everything possible to turn the world away from evil."

"How do we do that?" I asked.

"We will face many small battles. Jonah has collected an army. It's a gang of his choosing. It's only a matter of time before they try something. Fisher, you must begin training the students in your class to use their powers. You, also, must collect an army.

"Will I be able to use my mouth to talk to them?" I asked. "It would be easier to train them if I could use my mouth to talk."

Michael smiled, "Don't worry. They can all talk in their heads as you do. That will be of great use to you all in battle."

My head was swimming. How could I train all the kids in my class? How could I do it without anyone seeing us? Millions of pictures flew through my head. I felt a little dizzy, and kind of sick in my stomach.

"I will help," Michael said. He could see I was concerned. "Right now, just start by teaching one or two people at a time. Mary, Samuel and David can also help. They are already very powerful. Don't worry so much Fisher. Live each moment as it comes. You will find the answers to everything if you cherish each moment. Most people do not know how to do that. I nodded my head in agreement. This time, instead of walking through my wall, Michael just vanished. I blinked. It was just like the old episodes of Star Trek my dad and I watched, where people get all fuzzy, then disappear. Maybe I could also learn to just vanish. But, that would have to wait. I had lots of planning to do.

Daily Battles

I thought a lot about Michael's talk with me. He spoke of how the world was already turning into the netherworld, which is bad. Since his talk, I have noticed more bad things happening when I am on the internet looking at news.

Many people seem to be trying to tell everybody how to live their lives. It is happening a lot in the United States. Some people want everyone to believe in God the way they do. Some people do not like black people, and they think everyone should think that way. Some people do not like Muslims. I'm not really sure where Muslims come from, but there are many of them. Maybe there is a country called Muslinia, or something. Dad knows a Muslim family. Their

daughter plays in dad's middle school band. I met them after dad's last band

concert, and they acted very nice, I thought. Many people are also mad about gay

people. At first, I just though gay meant they were very happy, but dad explained

it. Dad says our neighbor lady, Rebecca, is gay, and she is very kind to me. She

never looks at me funny, or stares at me like I'm a freak the way some people do.

Maybe, like me, she knows how it feels to be an outsider.

I don't keep up with our government much, but dad talks about it a lot. He

says we have two main groups of people in government-Democrats and

Republicans. (Sometimes he calls the Democrats *idiots*, and the Republicans

really big idiots.) Dad says that both sides just want to prove THEY are right and

the other side is wrong. So nothing ever gets done, and people who are just

trying to make a living suffer, along with the poor people.

I think most of these problems could be talked about, but nobody seems to

want to sit down and talk. Most people I see on the news are fighting. I hope I

don't have to get into a fight with Jonah, or anybody else.

Famous people seem to be very unhappy. At the store, I see many

magazines about celebrities. They are always getting divorced, or breaking up, or going into the hospital because they use drugs. It is hard to find famous people who are happy. My dad says some people make a living by just being in those magazines and pretending to be famous. He says they just like to get in the magazines, because they are in love with themselves, and people buy the magazines, and make the phony people rich. That is a strange way to live. I read about one lady who makes millions of dollars every time she breaks up with a man. I feel bad for people who don't really learn to care for people or have anyone who cares about them. They must hurt a lot inside from being all alone.

Getting Organized

The next day, we were having movie time as a reward for good behavior. We were watching "How to Train Your Dragon." (The first one, not the second one...I don't like the second one because the dad dies.) While the movie played, Samuel, Mary and I were busy planning. We talked in our heads...

"How can we get the whole class together and practice our powers?" I asked.

Samuel had an idea, "My birthday party is a week from Saturday. I was going to invite the whole class to come over for the afternoon anyway. I live next to the old airplane factory. We could sneak in there to practice." He glanced back at the movie..."Oooh, I like this part where Hiccup finds the dragon he shot down in the woods!"

Mary added, "That's a great idea! There is a lot of space in the old airplane factory! There are also lots of things we could practice moving and throwing...I wonder if Toothless is a slimy dragon, or if he has smooth skin. I think he is nice and smooth, like leather. I bet he is

soft."

"I think it would be so cool to have retractable teeth like Toothless," I added. "Okay...Samuel, you need to get those invitations out and we will use that as a training day. Do

you guys think dragons have to sleep a lot? I mean, are they like dogs and sleep a whole lot, or do they fly around most of the time?"

Samuel said, "I think they are more like bats. They like to be awake at night and sleep in a cave during the day. Do you guys want to have pizza at my party, or should my mom have cake?"

"You have to have cake," said Mary. "It's your birthday!" "I wonder how Hiccup drags all those fish through the woods to feed Toothless? Don't you think that many fish would be heavy? "

"I don't know," I said. "He is a pretty skinny little guy. Are there still any old airplanes in the factory Samuel?"

"Yeah," he answered. "There are a few. Oh, I like this part! Toothless is going to take off and fly with Hiccup on his back! Then, they both fall into the lake!"

I was happy to hear there were still some old planes in the factory. This gave me an idea.

Samuel's Birthday Party

At Samuel's birthday party, nine students from our class showed up, along with me and Mary. To our surprise, David lived close to Samuel, so he joined us. Our parents dropped us off, and Samuel's mom and dad had some games for us, and birthday cake. After a while, we started to run around the yard on our own, so Samuel's parents went inside. They had a yard with a fence around it, because they had an old dog named Boswell. He was an old beagle. I liked him, because he wasn't wiggly like my dogs. After a while, Samuel told his parents we were going to play in the ball field behind the airplane factory. Mary was the oldest, so she promised Samuel's parents she would watch us, and we would stay in the ball field. Of course, this wasn't true. Once we got to the ball field, and were out of sight, we slipped into the old factory through a broken door Samuel knew about.

The old factory was a wonderful place. It was still full of old tools and machines, and even some airplanes. It had great big rooms that we could practice in. All of the other kids wanted to know what Samuel, Mary and I had to show them. I started by making an old hammer fly through the air. I had shown Mary and Samuel how to use the power when they visited my house, so they started moving tools around too. The other kids were amazed. Their mouths dropped open. I was the only one who could not talk, so they all started shouting.

"WOW!" They screamed. "Do something bigger!

Mary lifted a giant tool chest. She made it spin around three times, and fly over the other kids' heads. Samuel really amazed them by making himself lift about three feet into the air. Then, he raised his hand and made an old window open up.

The other kids all wanted to learn how to make things move right away, so we started teaching them. They were fast learners. Pretty soon, tools were flying everywhere. Doors were opening and slamming shut. David saw a tiny mouse crawling along the wall. He gently lifted it through the air and made it land in the palm of his hand.

David had a special quality about him. He seemed to have great powers. Michael had said he was the king of our tribe, and was the strongest, but he preferred to be very gentle and kind. He smiled a lot and seemed to be very happy. He wasn't at all scared like he had been with his bad dad at the store. He petted the mouse in his hand and talked to it. Then, he very gently out it back down on the floor and watched it crawl away. David was powerful and gentle at the same time.

I decided it was time to do something really big. Soon, Samuel's parents would be looking for us. I went over to an old airplane and got in the pilot's seat. In my head, I told everyone to hurry and get in. We could barely fit into the old plane. It was just the body, seats and wings. There were no engines or windows.

"Everyone be quiet," I said mentally. "We don't have much time. Clear your heads and concentrate on lifting the plane. Everyone breathe in and count to 5, then breathe out and count backwards back down to one."

Everyone got silent. You could hear the breathing. Even though nobody was counting out loud, I could feel the counting in my body. We were all in perfect rhythm together.

"Do it again," I spoke with my head. "Now everyone raise your hands."

The old shell of a plane began to shake and creak. Everyone let out a gasp. The plane stopped moving. We all got quiet, and went back to breathing in and out, and counting silently, with our hands high in the air. Sure enough...the old plane lifted about two feet off the floor.

"Now, think about moving forward," I thought.

The plane started to fly forward. It knocked over some tool cabinets.

"Higher," Mary yelled. "Think higher!"

The plane went almost to the ceiling and rushed forward. We almost slammed into a wall, but we all thought about turning, and the plane followed our thoughts. We went in big circles around the old factory.

"Think backwards," yelled Samuel.

The plane stopped and slowly flew in reverse. David had a look of joy on his face. He was really enjoying flying. In fact, everyone looked so happy. I think part of that was because it was just a lot of fun, but I also think it was because none of us felt like we had disabilities anymore. We had great abilities that nobody else had. We were like superheroes!

We finally thought about landing. It wasn't too gentle, but nobody got hurt. The plane slowly got lower and lower. When we were about three feet off the floor, the plane crashed down. Everyone screamed, but it was a happy, triumphant scream. Years of frustration at what our bodies and brains could not do vanished. We felt like nothing was impossible. We felt like a very special family.

As we turned to go out the door, we were startled. Michael was there. He had been watching. He smiled.

"You all did very well," he said proudly. "You had all better get back to Samuel's house. His parents will be looking for you soon."

The kids who had never met Michael before stood there with mouths open wide.

"You're blue!" One kid exclaimed. "And your eyes are huge! You must be an alien!"

"No, I think he is some kind of angel," said a girl. "I hear angels can just appear out of nowhere."

He smiled at me as I walked past him. He held out his fist and we exchanged a knuckle bump.

"Well done Fisher," he said. "Your mom is very proud of you right now."

He reached out his open hand. In it was a locket. My mom had been buried with that locket! It had a picture of her holding me when I was a baby.

"How did you get this?! I shouted in my head.

"I talk to your mom quite often," he said. "She is fine. She's always watching out for you. She wants you to keep this with you always for protection."

"Michael!" I looked at him with burning eyes. "Who or what are you? Are those kids right? Are you an alien, or maybe an angel?!"

"I have been called both of those things," he said. "Remember when I told you there are many dimensions to this universe?"

I nodded my head.

"I used to be a person like you," he continued. "I chose to live a life in the Behira tribe...doing good, and trying to love, and help others. The rewards of living that life are very great. If you live that way in your human life, you grow into a stronger being with many wonderful powers."

I remembered my lessons from Sunday school. Finally, I dared to ask.

"Are you the one they called the Archangel Michael?"

Just as I finished that thought, I turned and looked. Michael had indeed transformed into a giant angel, almost 7 feet tall. His skin was black now, like Samuel's. His head was still smooth, like my dad's bald head, but his eyes were emerald green, and he had a chin beard. He wore a long black coat. He removed the coat to reveal huge wings...with feathers and everything. They were also black, and extended almost to the ground.

"I though angels had white wings," I said.

"No, we're all different colors, just like people," Michael said. "Many ages ago, I fought in the war of angels...good against evil. When the Choshek were defeated, they began to create evil on Earth. Every faith on Earth speaks of a place of despair and evil."

"I always thought that was a place down below us... full of fire," I stated.

Michael explained, "Imagine the Earth with no parks...no trees or grass or water... a harsh brutal world, with no air to breathe, and no animal or plant life. Yes, it WOULD be very hot and fiery. The wealthy and powerful in this world, the Choshek, want to destroy all of the Earth's blessings to make even more money, and become even more powerful. They won't stop until there is nothing left, and the world will be miserable, painful, and without beauty."

"I understand now," I couldn't help but smile as I conveyed this thought to him, because I was looking at my mom's locket. "Please tell mom I said hello, and I love her."

Michael smiled back and nodded. He patted my shoulder and vanished. I stood there holding the locket. I felt weak, but full of joy. This universe was indeed a wonderful place. I had a lot to learn about it, and my education was just beginning. **Noah and Ruth**

Of all the new kids we trained, two stood out above the others. They were Noah and Ruth. Noah is one of the funniest people I have ever known. Jonah hates Noah. I think it is because Noah never lets Jonah's comments bother him. I think Jonah also hates Noah because Noah is Jewish. Jonah seems to hate anyone who does not think like he does.

Noah has thick glasses, red curly hair and a few extra pounds. He also has Asperger's Syndrome. It is a kind of autism. Noah is really smart. He reads all the time, and he likes to write. He can talk, but sometimes things don't always seem to fit in with what everyone else is saying. This just makes him funnier to me. In spite of this, he always seems to have a snappy come back for anything Jonah says. One time Jonah was trying to make Noah mad in class. Jonah made a comment about Noah's weight. Noah didn't even stop reading his book.

He kept reading and said, "Just more of me for the women to love."

Everyone laughed, except Jonah.

Ruth is also very funny. She is almost completely deaf. She has to wear great big hearing aids in both ears. They look uncomfortable, but Ruth is always happy. She acts as if every day is the best day ever. Ruth seems to have very strong powers. I think maybe it is because she has trouble hearing. She is able to block out things, and really concentrate. One day, at my house, she lifted herself in the air and sat for a long time meditating. She looked like a Buddhist monk. She sat that way while the dogs ran underneath her barking, but she never lost her concentration. Ruth is very quiet and usually kind, but likes to tell jokes and sometimes she goes too far and makes people upset. She and Mary are best friends.   **More Training**

After our success at the old airplane factory, we all felt great, but we had to find a way to keep practicing in secret. We did this by taking turns going to visit each other. Sometimes, several of us would meet at Mary's house. We would rotate around to Samuel's house and then my house. All of our houses had basements with plenty of room. Things went very well this way; although, one time, Mary's mom surprised us when she came downstairs to do laundry. She almost saw Samuel making the cat's litter box fly through the air, but Mary jumped in front of her to block it from her vision. Our powers were very strong now. There were twelve of us. I hoped we weren't getting too confident, but it really did feel great to have super ability, rather than thinking we were "disabled."   **The Battles Begin**

One day, Mary, Samuel and I were walking downtown. My dad usually went everywhere with me, but now he kind of saw Mary as my big sister, so he let her take me places. It was a warm day, but there were dark clouds coming in. The air was thick. I hate it when the weather is like that, because it seems to make a lot of sounds louder to me. The noise from the traffic was really bothering me. I put on my headphones to help block the noise. I felt uneasy and tense, but I didn't know why. I kept my mom's locket in my pocket all the time. I squeezed it. It made me feel calmer.

We walked behind the post office into an alley. Since I had my headphones on, I was really shocked when Mary and Samuel both pushed me behind a wall. I pulled the headphones off and looked at them with big eyes.

"What's wrong with you?!" I shouted mentally.

They both pointed down to the corner. There, behind an old abandoned store, were several large boys, all dressed in black. They were holding another boy and taking turns punching him in the stomach. Another boy stood in front of them and watched. It was Jonah. The boy they were holding was someone I had seen at school. I think his name was Eli. He was twisting and

pulling- trying to get away, of course, but three boys held him. I could see his mouth was bleeding.

He yelled, "I gave you the money, now leave me alone!"

Blood poured out of his mouth as he spoke.

"You only gave me half," said Jonah. He pulled out a long knife. "I'm gonna cut the rest out of you I guess."

Jonah smiled as he put the knife to Eli's throat. Eli gave out a terrified shriek.

"Come on Jonah," said one of the gang members. "If he had any more money, he would have given it to you. We need to get out of here before the cops come."

As fast as lightning, Jonah waved his hand at the member of his gang, and the kid flew back into the wall.

"Anybody else in a hurry?!" Jonah yelled at his gang.

The gang members stood silently. They were afraid of Jonah. They didn't even blink their eyes.

"Mary, What are we gonna...?" I started to ask in my head.

Before I could even finish the thought, I saw Jonah's hand drop the knife. He screamed in pain and clutched his stomach.

"Oh God...What's happening?! Jonah yelled. He started writhing on the ground, and making horrible painful sounds.

His terrified gang members let go of Eli.

"We'd better get out of here!" another gangster yelled.

Before any of them could move, the wind started to blow in huge gusts. A window on the old building broke, and glass flew everywhere. The dumpster the gangsters stood beside flipped completely over and spun in circles, as if it were in the middle of a tornado. A street light shattered above them, and sparks flew down on Jonah. The whole gang screamed like little girls. I looked over at Mary and Samuel to see if they were doing any of this, but they just stood there motionless, looking as confused as everyone else. I saw Jonah lifted into the air. He was spinning around like a top. His gang members covered their ears as a loud shriek blasted all around us. It sounded like a wild animal in pain, but hundreds of times louder than any I had ever heard. The noise felt like a hot needle going into my brain. I put my headphones back on.

As suddenly as it had started, it stopped. Eli had run off long ago. All of the gang members ran away as fast as they could. Jonah slowly and cautiously looked around. Nothing was there. He was completely alone. Deserted by his gang, he picked up his knife and ran off

"What in the world was that?!" asked Samuel.

"Dunno," answered Mary.

I took my headphones off again, and the three of us slowly came out from behind the wall we had been hiding behind. Inch by inch, we headed toward the spot where this had all taken place. We relaxed slightly. Mary and I cautiously walked over and looked at the dumpster. It was flattened like an old piece of aluminum foil. Mary picked up pieces of broken glass from the broken streetlight and the window.

Hey guys!" Samuel said in his normally quiet voice. "Take a look at who I found."

Mary and I turned. Our mouths dropped open. Samuel looked at us with an awe-inspired grin. There, standing by a huge elm tree, with a big smile on his face, was little tiny David.

Jonah Disappears

The next day in school, we were all surprised to see the police in our classroom with our teachers. Everyone looked very serious. Mr. Kleiner asked us all to take our seats.

"This is Trooper Ramirez," Mr. Kleiner said. "He needs to speak with you, so please give him all of your attention."

We all felt scared. Nobody knew what had happened. The trooper told us that

the night before, Jonah and his dad had gotten into a big fight. Jonah's dad was

dead. Jonah had killed his own father! There was complete silence in the room.

We all looked at each other. We all knew Jonah was bad, but I don't think anyone

thought he would actually kill someone, especially his own dad.

The trooper told us that the police were not sure where Jonah was, and that we

all needed to call right away if we saw him. He asked if anyone had any idea

where Jonah might go, but none of us said a word. We never really spent much

time around Jonah, because we all knew what he was like. I began to wonder if

Jonah had used his powers to kill his dad. Maybe he didn't mean to kill him, but

his powers had gotten out of control. The rest of the day was very quiet. Some

people I didn't know said they just knew Jonah would do something like this

someday.

I heard two women teachers talking.

"He's always been bad, and it was just a matter of time," one said to the

other.

I remembered these two teachers. They had always said bad things about

Jonah. Jonah had always said he would "get them" someday.

"At least it doesn't look like he will be our problem anymore," said the other woman.

I felt bad. Many people seemed to be almost happy that Jonah had done this terrible thing. I never liked how Jonah acted, but I had always hoped that he might change someday. Everyone in my class felt pretty sad too. Jonah was mean and bad, but he was one of us. He was a special ed. kid. We all worried that this might make everyone look down on all of us special ed. kids.

Nerves

That day after school, I paced a lot. I started to shake my hands too. It was bad, because I started to feel like I wasn't special anymore. I started to feel like the word Jonah had always used...a "sped," or worse yet, a "retard." I felt guilty in a way. I learned that I had these special powers, and I had kind of started to think I was better than everyone else. All my life, people had stared at me, made comments about me, and sometimes even crossed the street to avoid me. Now, I felt like I was bad for having powers nobody else had. Had I gotten too carried away? Jonah really didn't like me. What if his anger at me, and all my friends, had been part of the reason he killed his dad?

My nerves got worse. I felt sick to my stomach. I was shaking and sweating. I sat down on a chair and started to rock back and forth. Usually, that really calms me down. This time, it didn't work. I let out a terrible groan. My dad came running in. He knew that yell. It was the noise I made when I was unable to calm down, and I was trying to scream for help. I was mad. I hated my autism for keeping me from yelling like a normal person. I just wanted to tell my dad my problems like any other kid could!

Dad ran to the kitchen. He got my liquid medicine, and shot some of it down my throat. He tried to hug me. Normally, I wanted him to give me a hug, but not this time. I pulled away and went back to pacing and flapping my hands.

"What is it buddy? He said. "Are you sick? Do you hurt?"

Dad went through all the standard questions he used when I was upset. He took both my hands and held them for a while. He rubbed the top of my head really hard. We always called a certain spot on top my head "the autism spot." Dad would rub it when I was stressed. It always helped bring me back down. He also ran a hand up and down my back to soothe me.

At last, I could feel the meds working. Gradually, I was calming down. Dad asked if I had just had a bad dream. I nodded my head. I decided that was as good a reason as any. I didn't want him to worry anymore. Finally, I reached my arms around him and gave him a hug. Everything was better.

I realized as I hugged him that he was my life, and I was his. He didn't have mom anymore for support. We had each other, and that was enough. At that moment, I felt very warm and content. It wasn't the medicine so much. It was the hug. I really started to relax. I realized that my dad got strength from me, and I needed to stay strong for him. I held him tightly. Even though it was just me and dad, we were a family...a kind of comical and weird

family, but we were strong. Maybe that was the real reason I had autism. It was because dad and I were strong enough together to handle it. We were a team. However, just as Michael had said, the time had come for the people like me to rise up and become leaders.   **Silence**

The next couple of days were very quiet in many ways. First of all, nobody knew where Jonah had gone. The police had been hanging around the school, hoping somebody would have some news, or information about where he was. I suspected that, like me and all my "army," Jonah could vanish, or at least walk through walls. We had all mastered that by now, so I was sure Jonah had too. That ability would make him impossible to find.

The whole school was quieter than normal, especially in our classroom. Everyone had Jonah on his or her mind. Even Mr. Kleiner was quiet, and hardly anything ever bothered him. I think a lot of the regular ed. kids thought we were covering up for Jonah, but they were wrong. We all wanted Jonah to be caught. He might come after any one of us. I was especially worried about Samuel. Jonah hated Sam so much. I think maybe Jonah had come to hate Sam even more than he hated me.

That night, I sat in silence in my bed, in complete darkness. I tried to clear my head of the pictures that usually flew at me. At first, I had no luck. Then, I tried counting and breathing the way I did when I moved objects. It worked. I was able to clear my head. Since that worked so well, I decided to lift myself off the bed in a sitting position. There I sat, like a Buddhist monk, two feet above my bed. Michael had told me that breathing was important to Buddhists...a source of peace and strength. I sat there, just concentrating on my breathing. I slowly lowered and raised myself a few times. It was so silent and peaceful. I was actually learning to control my autism sometimes. That moment was the most peaceful one of my life.

The Confrontation

The next day, things felt slightly more normal at school. Everyone was in a better mood. Mary asked Noah, Ruth, Sam and I to walk to her house after school. Mr. Kleiner had called my dad to get the OK. Dad agreed. He told Mr. Kleiner to tell Mary he would pick me up at Mary's house around five o'clock.

We were walking through a big field by an old abandoned store. It was a shortcut to Mary's house. Noah was kicking a can to Sam, and Sam would kick it back to Noah. Everyone felt happy and relaxed. Maybe Jonah had run away since he was in so much trouble. He could probably stay hidden forever by using his powers. As we got close to the old store, Noah picked up the can, and threw it through the broken window into the old building. We turned toward Mary's house, and the can came shooting back at us. We all looked at each other. We immediately knew who was in the old building.

Mary spoke bravely. "Come on out Jonah. This has gone too far!"

Sam got very nervous. He could feel hostility and pure hatred coming from inside the old store.

"Jonah! Mary yelled louder. "Just stop! We can help you!"

As Mary inched closer to the old store, we heard Jonah speak.

"Stay right there where I can see all of you," he said.

"Jonah," said Mary, we don't want to fight. We want to help you. We will go with you if you will just turn yourself in to the police."

Jonah wasn't having any of it. He and several of his gang members came running out of the old store right at us. Jonah raised his hands at me, and I went flying backwards about ten feet, landing on my back. The force of hitting the ground knocked the wind out of me. Mary watched me hit the ground, and got very red in the face. One of Jonah's gang raced right at her. She jumped over him. After he got past her, he spun around looking confused. Mary literally left her feet and flew at him like a jet, knocking him to the ground by hitting him in the face with both fists. The kid was out cold.

Jonah grabbed the back of my shirt and threw me several feet. I landed on the rock-hard ground. I was trying not to get angry, but it was tough. Every time my anger increased, my powers weakened. He kicked me in the stomach. It hurt pretty badly. I gasped and grabbed his leg. I stood up fast and spun him around in circles. Finally, I let go and he shot through the air, and smacked into a tree.

Jonah shook off the pain. He turned to watch his gang. Noah and Ruth were busy chasing two other gang members. I couldn't believe it. Here were two quiet, timid, life skills kids, yelling at the top of their lungs, and running full steam after two scared punks. The gang members had knives, but Noah used his powers to knock them out of the boys' hands. Ruth had a large stick. She was using her powers to spin the stick around and around like a propeller. Every time Jonah's boys slowed down, it smacked them in the butt.

Mary was still trying to stop the whole thing. "This is STUPID! STOP! Stop Jonah, before you kill another person!"

Jonah wouldn't stop. He was going right for Samuel. He kicked Sam in the shins and knocked him down. Samuel yelled in pain. Jonah waved his arm and a large rock came flying right at Sam's head. I didn't even have time to think. I held up my hand and stopped the rock in mid-air. Jonah held up his hand and the rock came at my head. Again, I stopped it. By this time, Sam was back on his feet, but he was hurt and limping. I could see that he was in pain. He looked furious at Jonah. I knew he couldn't lose his temper, or Jonah would win, and probably kill him. Jonah waved his hand and the rock once again sped toward Samuel.

"Sam, just lay down!" I screamed in my head.

Sam did, and the rock missed his head by an inch. By this time, he had remembered that he had to calm down. Still sitting on the ground, Samuel closed his eyes, and held one hand up at Jonah. Slowly, Jonah lifted into the air. Sam held him there for several seconds, until Jonah threw a knife at Sam. Sam slid sideways. The knife just missed him, but he lost his concentration, and Jonah fell back to the ground.

I remembered we were on an old ballfield by the abandoned store. The ground was nothing but sand, rocks, broken glass, and loose dirt. I thought of how David had used his power to make the wind blow the dumpster over. I twirled my hands in circles over and over again. It worked! I had started a small tornado of dirt, rocks and glass. It was spinning at Jonah. He yelled in pain and closed his eyes tightly.

I kept the circles going. The tornado picked up Jonah and lifted him twenty feet in the air. I stopped twirling my hands and he landed with a loud thud. It sounded like every bone in his body had broken. His eyes were closed and he wasn't moving.

"Oh no!" I thought. "I've killed him! Now the police will be after me!" Everyone stopped fighting and looked at Jonah, motionless on the ground. His gang members ran and limped off the field. The two kids that Noah and Ruth had been chasing ran screaming into the woods.

"See what happens when you make the Jew kid mad?!" yelled Noah.

Ruth smiled and patted him on the back. Throughout the entire fight, Ruth had not lost her cool. For someone who was always so sweet, she was a fierce fighter. In fact, I think she may have enjoyed it a little.

We all ran over to Sam. He was still down on the ground. His left leg was bleeding. We lifted him up slowly. He could walk.

"I don't think it's busted," he said. "You OK Mary?"

Mary looked more upset than the rest of us. "Why did they have to do that?" She started to cry a little. "Why can't he just stop this craziness?"

"Maybe he's just mad at the world," Ruth answered.

"Well, I'm gonna ask him!" Mary hissed through clenched teeth. She spun around toward Jonah, but he was gone! How could this be?

"He wasn't even moving a second ago," Sam said.

"With any luck, he evaporated," quipped Noah.

I stood there stunned. I thought I'd killed Jonah, but somehow, he had vanished.

Apparently, someone had seen the fight and called the police. Police cars were pulling in from all directions.

When the officers got to us, Mary told them how we had been walking past, and Jonah's gang attacked us.

"And you guys beat them in a fight?" the stunned officer asked.

"We don't look so tough, but we're actually Ninja trainees," Noah said. "Ruth here is an animal."

Ruth just stood and smiled. Sam told the officers that Jonah and his gang had all run into the woods.

The police simply stood there looking at us. They got into a huddle and talked softly for a minute. Then, one came back over to us.

"Kids, please don't take this the wrong way, but we're just having a hard time with this," the officer said nervously.

"Why is that?" smiled Sam.

"Well," one of the other officers said. "It's just a little tough to figure how these really, uh...bad kids got stomped on by a bunch of..."

"What my partner is trying to say," a woman officer interrupted, "is that you guys are some pretty amazing kids, but you DO happen to have some, uh...special qualities about you?"

"You mean we're retards?" said Ruth with a smile.

We all looked at Ruth with our mouths dropped open. Sweet little Ruth, who never said a bad word about anyone, had just used the big "R" bomb…TO THE POLICE!!!

"OK, the officer in charge said. "I think we've held you kids up long enough. We're going to go start searching for these guys."

He looked at Sam, "You okay buddy? We can give you a lift home. Or do you need to go to the hospital?"

"I'm just fine officer," Sam replied. "Thank you kindly, but I'll walk."

We all started to walk away together. The officers were talking quietly again. We couldn't really hear much, then one of them spoke a little louder.

"Man, don't mess with those kids!"

The police all took off to look for Jonah and his gang. We were all a little rattled, but we also felt pretty good. We went to Mary's house and got ourselves cleaned up. Mary's mom and dad came home from work, and we all sat down to a big spaghetti dinner. It was a simple dinner, but it tasted incredibly good.

Peace

That night I lay in my bed in the dark. I felt incredibly relaxed considering what

had happened that day. I sat up in my meditation position again, did my

breathing, and slowly lifted into the air, and closed my eyes. Hovering two feet

above my bed, I realized how much I had changed since Michael had come into

my life. My whole group of friends had changed radically. Aside from our new

powers, we were all braver, funnier, calmer and much more confident. Words

came so much more clearly to me now, and my writing and typing had improved.

Mr. Kleiner had noticed it. I had actually started to really appreciate the animals

more...even the dogs. Food tasted better to me. I'd have to say that I had a much

greater love of life. To be honest, I don't think any of this had to do with my

actual "new" powers. I think Michael had opened up my mind to a whole new

appreciation of life. I think most people sadly live their lives in a tunnel. They go

through the same motions each day, never really using the creative side of their

brains to look outward and see new possibilities and opportunities. Michael had

taught all of us that we had great powers, even without all the magic stuff. Ruth

had an incredible brain, and an amazing sense of humor. David was small but had

the power of a giant. Mary had unlimited love and patience. Sam was fearless.

Those things had always been there, but we never looked for them. I

concentrated hard and turned myself upside down, still in a sitting position. I let my brain wander as blood flowed to my head. Maybe every person on Earth has amazing powers and abilities, but didn't know how to put them into use. Maybe people had lost the ability to look for the shining light they all had. Every day, I hear of somebody who can do something amazing. Maybe if everyone could get out of their personal tunnel, they could find their powers.

I opened my eyes and looked down at my cat, Edward, asleep directly below my head. I blew gently at him. He opened his eyes, hissed at me, and took off out of the room. That made me laugh. I lost my concentration and fell onto my bed. I sat up and continued with my thoughts. I watched a movie with dad once...one of his favorites. In it, the people in heaven used all of their brains. Most of the people just getting to heaven from Earth only used ten percent of their brains. The people in heaven jokingly referred to them as "little brains." Maybe, that's true. It's not about being dumb. It's about opening up our brains to see our own powers. We have to get out of our tunnels.

A Dark Day

It started out like any other day at school. We said the pledge and had a moment of silence. We started or morning work. Things were completely normal until about 10:00 that morning. The Principal came over the loudspeaker and calmly said we should stay in our classrooms. He also instructed all the teachers to lock their doors and windows. Mr. Kleiner did this and turned out the lights too. We all huddled in the corner of the room that was away from the door and windows. We were in a lockdown. We had practiced this a few times, but never thought much of it. Maybe this was just another practice…probably. We hadn't done one in a long time.

"I'm hungry Mr. Kleiner…" Noah started to joke, but he stopped when he saw the look Mr. Kleiner gave him. That look said it all. This was no drill. There was a big problem in our school. Everyone started to look pretty scared. Mary held my hand.

"Just stay very quiet," Mr. Kleiner whispered.

We stayed that way for almost two hours. We heard police sirens outside. In the distance, we could hear police talking over a loud speaker to someone. I thought I heard some women scream. Right away, I thought of Jonah. What had he done?

I heard noise in the hall. I stretched my neck way out when Mr. Kleiner wasn't looking in my direction. I knew it was dangerous, but I really wanted to see what was happening. State Troopers were running up and down the halls.

They were in SWAT uniforms and had machine guns and gas masks. I had seen

things like this happen on television, but it feels a lot creepier when it is

happening to you. I got that sick feeling back in my stomach. I really needed to

pace, but that was out of the question. I couldn't even flap my hands, or groan a

sound. It felt like my head would explode. Mr. Kleiner slowly rubbed my "autism

spot," and that helped. He's a big guy, so he could put a lot of pressure on it just

by using his thumb. Mary squeezed my hand hard, and I squeezed hers. We

heard some shots in the distance. A couple of people in my room started to

scream, but Mr. Kleiner reminded them that they HAD to be quiet.

It got completely silent in our hallway. I figured either something really

good was about to happen, or something really awful. Finally, the police were

moving in the hallway again. There was no talking, but they were rushing kids and

teachers out of the building. Everyone was walking very quickly in a long straight

line. They came to our room, and we joined the line. We all felt really scared, but

we stayed super quiet, and got out the door. When we got to the door, some

officers told us to run to the football field.

As soon as we hit the football field, I saw lots of parents standing there looking very worried. They were grabbing their kids and hugging them. I heard my name from behind me. I spun around and saw my dad running toward me. We gave each other a big hug.

The troopers told us to sit in the stands while they accounted for everybody. Teachers and Principals were counting kids and talking to parents. We all started to think we could go home soon when we heard more shooting. The trooper SWAT team had the cafeteria building surrounded, so I felt safe way up at the football field. Snipers were on the roof. Police were kneeling behind their cars, with the lights on top flashing. My dad asked an officer who was still inside the building.

"It's that kid we were looking for, Jonah Robertson," the trooper replied. "He's holding two women hostage."

"Do you know who they are?" Dad asked.

"All I know is they are teachers," the trooper replied.

I knew it! Jonah was holding those two women at gun point...the two women who were always saying bad things about him!

I started to think hard about what my dad had always said...how we need to help those who are suffering. What was the right thing to do here? Jonah was a bad kid, absolutely no doubt about it. He had chosen to be bad, even when people like Mr. Kleiner had tried to help him.

Just then, a state trooper walked over to us.

"Is there a girl named Mary here? He asked.

Mary stepped forward. "That's me."

"This kid Jonah wants to talk to you on the phone." The trooper looked disgusted with the whole situation. "Mary, you don't have to talk to him if you don't want to, but if you can help us get him out of there, I'd really be grateful," he said.

Mary agreed to talk to Jonah.

"I'll put him on the speaker phone," the trooper said.

We all clustered around Mary for moral support. I felt useless. I couldn't talk. What was I going to be able to do? Then I realized, Mary was my best friend. She held my hand when we were so scared in the classroom. The least I could do was to stand by her now. Ruth, Noah, and even Sam went over with Mary and I to the speaker phone.

"Jonah...Are you there?" Mary asked timidly.

The trooper whispered to us, "He got shot in the shoulder by a sniper a while ago. He's probably getting weak."

"Shot!?" Mary's voice sounded angry and worried at the same time.

The trooper explained, "He was pointing his rifle at one of the hostages."

Finally, Jonah answered. "Yeah, I'm still here."

"Jonah," continued Mary, "It's not too late. Please just come out before anybody else gets hurt."

I figured Jonah was getting desperate. His powers probably wouldn't work because he was in pain and couldn't concentrate.

"What do I have to lose, Miss Mary?" Jonah said kind of sarcastically. It's not like my future looks real peachy. I should probably just end this now by blowing me, and these two old cows away!" Jonah sounded really mad.

Mary was quiet for a long time. Then she went on, "Jonah...Why do you hate everyone so much?! What made you this mad? We all just wanted to be your friends."

There was silence...nothing but the sound of Jonah's labored breathing, and an occasional whimper from one of the ladies being held hostage.

"I never learned to care about anyone," Jonah finally said. "My old man treated me like dirt because I had one stupid little disability!"

Mary tried to sound calm and soothing, "I never knew why you were in our class Jonah. None of us did. You always seemed to be...uh...normal."

"Autism!" Jonah yelled. "Friggin' autism! That's what I have. I couldn't talk until I was seven years old! You would have thought I was from Mars the way my dad treated me. He'd get real drunk and call me a retard! He'd hit me and tell me I was worthless and stupid. He always blamed me for mom leaving. Sometimes, he'd even lock me in a room and leave for a couple of days! Then, he'd come back all nice and try to make it up to me by buying me stuff. Then, a couple of days later, it would all start again."

Everyone was silent. Then Jonah started in again.

"One good thing though. I guess the old man beat it out of me, cuz it barely shows now. I suppose I shoulda' thanked him for that before I killed him."

Ruth spoke up, "Jonah? Why don't you let those ladies go? They don't matter."

"Oh, Ruthy…You're getting awful brave." Jonah was screaming now. "They sure do matter! These are the two wenches who were always bad-mouthin' me. Every day…talkin' about what a bad kid I was, and how I should be locked away so I wouldn't inconvenience them anymore!"

We could all tell Jonah was trying to stand up from his grunting and heavy breathing. He was getting weak from the loss of blood from his gunshot wound.

"Jonah!" Noah decided to try. "There are people who can help you! Don't make it worse! Just come out with your hands up! Go with the police. So what if you have to be locked up for a while? People want to help you! You can still get your life back"

Jonah wasn't having it. "I think what I need to do is finish this myself, starting with these two old goons I got right here! I'm gonna' start blasting!

A police radio sounded, "Sniper four… I have a clear shot."

This was followed by another voice over the radio, "Take him."

We heard a shot. Then, we heard the two women scream. Then, there was no sound.

Police radios went crazy. We heard them everywhere.

"Subject is down."

"SWAT team move in. Subject is down...repeat, subject is down."

Police were storming the cafeteria wing.

We all stood helpless as the police ran in and out of the building, finally emerging with the two women teachers who had been held hostage. They were crying and very shaky, but did not seem to be hurt. There was no sign of Jonah.

Finally, the police radio sounded again, "We are bringing him out. We need a stretcher."

"A stretcher," I thought. What does that mean? Is he alive or dead?"

I looked at Mary. Tears were streaming down her face, but she was silent. Noah's face was always kind of blank, and without expression. Now, he looked as if he was in pain. That really made me think. Here was a kid who had always been picked on by Jonah. Noah had always kept his sense of humor, never letting

Jonah get to him. As nasty as Jonah had always been to Noah, Noah had never given up on him. I think Noah's quick come-backs had just been a way for Noah to say he cared. I remembered how Michael had said we had to try everything possible to turn Jonah around. I think of all of us, Noah had most believed that he could change Jonah. Ruth looked calm and strong. This whole experience of learning of our powers, and facing Jonah, had made Ruth into a true hero, full of bravery and confidence. I turned my head and looked over at Samuel. Sam was the most upset. He was actually weeping out loud.

"Why did this have to happen?" he said with anger in his voice. "Why can't people just live together and get along?"

After about thirty minutes, we saw people starting to come out of the building. Four members of the SWAT team surrounded Jonah on a stretcher. Even from a distance, we could see bloody bandages on Jonah's shoulders. He still hadn't moved, but maybe that was because he was strapped down so tightly. Too weak to fight, or use any of his powers, he finally turned his head and looked in our direction as the police loaded him into an ambulance. Two troopers and two medics got into the ambulance with him. State police cars escorted the ambulance out of the parking lot and off to the hospital.

Many people just got into cars and quietly left. Some people cried. Some said mean things about Jonah. I stood there with my little army. Nobody said anything. Dad came over to me, took my arm calmly, and led me to the car to go home. I felt helpless.

Aftermath

Things at school gradually calmed down and returned to normal, as much as possible. I think we all felt that our lives would never really be completely normal again though. We were different people now. Some people like to say that people never change, but I don't believe that. I'm very different now. The kids in my life skills class are much different now. Nobody says mean things anymore. Everyone tries to help one another. We work harder at our schoolwork. The regular ed. kids seem to accept us more now. They don't walk away from us or avoid us at lunch. A few of them even eat with us. We still have our powers, and we still get together to practice in secret. However, we don't seem to need our powers right now. Maybe we will someday. Right now, we have all found special power we didn't know we had. It's the power to be confident and proud.

Jonah is in a kind of prison for boys. None of us have ever gone to see him. We are all kind of scared to go. What if he acted crazy, or really mad at us? What if we said something that really made him feel bad? Then, after I ask myself those questions, I realize that those are the kinds of reasons most people have for not wanting to be around "special needs" people. They are afraid we might act crazy, or they might say something wrong. So, I think I will go see Jonah. I'm not sure when, but I think I should. It's just the right thing to do.

A year has passed and I have not seen Michael. However, a couple of times when I've been sitting out on the porch with dad in the dark, I am sure I've heard big wings flapping above the trees. Twice, I've gone into my bedroom to sleep, and found a gift on my desk...a large black feather. My angel buddy checks on me. I know it.

The End

Made in the USA
Middletown, DE
23 December 2020